CW00840217

This book belongs to:

....

For Anthony and Thea

POPPY OAK PRESS

An imprint of Pure Ink Press

Copyright © 2024 by Leila Summers
All rights reserved.

Paperback ISBN: 978-1-7764162-0-2
Ebook ISBN: 978-1-7764162-1-9

Contributing Author: Roger Pitot
Illustrated by Olesya Burina

www.pureinkpress.com
healinganagrams.com

CoCo
the
Mooing Horse

written by Leila Summers

illustrated by Olesya Burina

POPPY OAK PRESS

HUMOROUS
HEALING
ANAGRAMS

www.healinganagrams.com

HUMOROUS HEALING ANAGRAMS

A Note for Parents

Anagrams are words or phrases formed by rearranging the letters of other words or phrases. A true anagram uses all the letters in a word to make a new word. For example, "thing" can become "night" by rearranging and using all the letters.

However, the stories in Humorous Healing Anagrams make anagrams with any letters from a word or phrase. For example, by mixing up the letters in the word "night," you can make many other words, such as thing, hint, nigh, thin, ting, hit, nit, tin, hi, and it.

More than simply being entertaining, each story in the Humorous Healing Anagrams book series is created from words that are anagrams of the name of a specific common childhood issue and connected words or phrases. Mixing up the letters of the words that describe an "issue" creates other words. Using as many of the new words as possible, we can write a fun story (unrelated to the issue) that allows us to focus on something else—a different way of looking at things that makes us smile.

At the end of this book is a list of words that are anagrams of the phrase "common cold" and other connected words or phrases, including head cold, runny nose, sore throat, sneezing, congestion, headache, and coughing. We created *Coco the Mooing Horse* using as many words from the list as possible. We encourage children to write funny stories using words from this list as we did.

Once upon a time, on a farm that lay at the foot of a hill, there lived a rare old horse named Coco. His coat was the color of ash and coal, and he wore a retro hat and tie. He was a real gent.

Instead of neighing, he used to moo. His moos would echo across the farm. He said it was in his genes, but some said he was a loon and as mad as a hatter. After all, horses don't moo—cows do!

Each day at noon, he would sing and moo his rare ode to the sun. None of the other animals in earshot would take any notice, as they thought it was just an annoying noise.

But some of the cows thought it was cool that he tried to sound like them.

When the mood took him, he would moo so loudly that even the noisy rooster and the snooty goose would run and hide.

He didn't take any heed of them or let this hurt his ego, as he had made an oath to himself that he would resort to whatever it took to test his art of singing.

Although he'd heard that onions were good for the voice box, he thought they were odd and couldn't bear their scent or taste. Instead, he would eat sour rye, oats, and soy every day as a tonic to keep his voice strong.

When the sun set and the moon arose in the east, he would lie in his nest of hay like a cocoon on the earth and dream about becoming a singing star. As he slept, he would snore, making his chin wobble and his nose shake.

One hot, sunny day, he overheard a hare telling the rat about a sign she'd seen of a gig being hosted at a nearby inn. Coco decided he was going to seize the moment and enter the contest, as it only cost nine cents, which was a good deal.

He sent off a note to book his place in the singing section. The other animals mocked him and called him a crazy old coot. But he didn't need their consent and wouldn't let them shatter his dreams.

When the big day came, he ate his tonic, polished his horseshoes, put on his hat and tie, and trotted off in haste with his head held high.

At the inn, the animals all took their seats and waited for the talent show to begin.
First up was a cooing chicken, followed by a short hog who yodeled for eons.
Coco thought it was a bit dull, but then again, he'd never been into yodeling.

Just before it was his turn, an insect flew
into his throat, and he wished he had
some ice. When he got onto the stage
and tried to sing, he found his voice was
like tin, and he had to ask to restart.

This made the hare, goose, hog, otter, and other animals hoot with laughter. "Haha, that horse will get one out of ten!" they cried.

Coco was in a state and wanted to climb into a hole, but he told himself he had done this tons of times. He had to moo! He steadied his torso, rose up on his toes, put each ear back, gave a nod, and, in spite of the stares, made a new start. He let out the most beautiful, perfect moo he had ever mooed. It was a moo that came straight from the heart.

His song was so soothing and the tone so rare that the tension lifted, and there were many oohs and aahs from the lads and lasses. The hare and the rat stared at each other and said, "Gee, we didn't know he was such an ace." Even some of the judges were in tears and wanted another taste of his sonnets.

His next song was a real treat and soon brought toots and roars from all who could hear it. Afterward, a gnu in the crowd gave him a hug and said, "Son, you sound just like my old dad."

The nicest part was when the rooster brought him a plate loaded with toast, scones, tarts, and even cola, which made his heart soar.

The judges rated him a ten out of ten. He felt as if his name were in neon lights when he held his prize—a bag of coins!

Ever since that day, Coco has been a local icon and hero, and nobody has ever mocked his mooing again.

He would tell anyone who cared to listen that you can never see what is ahead or what is in store for you, so you should rather give it your best shot and shoot for a star!

Although many years have passed, the legend of Coco the mooing horse lives on, inspiring generations to hold fast to their dreams and follow their hearts.

THE END

From the Author

My name is Leila Summers. I am an author and book coach with a love for all things creative and human. I am also a trained Heal Your Life® teacher.

Louise Hay said that life is very simple. Every thought we think is creating our lives, and if we change our thoughts, we can change our lives. Simply put, the thoughts we think over and over become hardwired in our brains. These learned pathways in the brain can cause us to repeatedly recreate the same outcomes in our lives, even if those outcomes are not what we want. We can rewire our brains by changing our thoughts, which takes effort, commitment, and time.

Alexey Buchev, a Bulgarian psychologist, has a different and very interesting take on approaching problems and changing your mindset. I first came across Alexey's theories through an author I worked with, Ivinela Samuilova. In her bestselling book, *Life Can Be a Miracle*, Ivinela shares some of Alexey's unconventional and fun techniques for approaching problems in a completely different way to change how we perceive life and bring about a new reality.

One of the techniques I learned from Ivinela was how to use anagrams to approach a problem differently, particularly a physical illness. At the time, I had an incisional hernia from an old scar. Ivinela advised me to take the name of the illness and create anagrams from that phrase, then write a funny story using the words I came up with. At the end, she told me to choose one sentence from my story as a healing mantra and to say it out loud every time I felt pain.

From my story, I chose the sentence, "'That's insane,' said the snail." I must have said that hundreds of times during the months I awaited surgery. It allowed me to focus on something other than my pain and always made me smile. As it turned out, that, among other healing practices, helped me to heal my hernia before my surgery!

Another time, I was having issues at work, and I decided to write an anagram story using the title of the company. My mantra was, "Welcome to Sweden!" It really helped me to change my mood every time work got me down. And eventually, I was able to leave that job and try something new.

Whatever your issue might be, try it. You can learn many other great techniques from Ivinela's book, which is available on Amazon. I also explain everything in more detail on my website, www.healinganagrams.com.

Much love,

Write Your Own Story

On the following pages is a list of words that are anagrams of the phrase "common cold" and other phrases of symptoms related to the common cold.

Try writing your own funny story using as many of these words as possible. How many words can you use? Then go ahead and choose one sentence from your own story as your personal mantra. It can be any sentence you like. When you feel sick or miserable, say your mantra out loud. At the very least, it should make you smile. After all, they say that laughter is the best medicine!

Send your story to us for a chance to win a copy of one of the other books in the Humorous Healing Anagrams series.

Submit your story to www.healinganagrams.com/storysubmissions

Anagram Word List

aah	coal	coot	ego	gone
ace	coco	coots	egos	goo
add	cocoon	cost	engine	goon
ah	cod	costing	engines	goons
aha	coddle	cots	eon	goose
ahead	code	dad	eons	got
ale	coded	dead	gee	gun
are	cogs	deal	geez	ha
arose	coin	do	gene	had
arrest	coins	doom	genes	haha
art	cola	each	genie	halo
arts	con	ear	gent	hare
as	cons	ears	gents	hares
ash	consent	earshot	get	has
ashore	coo	earth	gets	haste
at	cooing	earths	gig	hat
ate	cool	east	gnu	hate
cent	coon	eat	go	hates
cents	coons	eats	goes	hats
chin	coos	echo	going	hatter

hatters	hoot	into	nest	note
he	hooter	is	nesting	notice
head	hooters	it	net	notices
heal	hoots	its	nets	noting
hear	horse	lace	nice	noun
hears	hose	laced	nicest	nouns
heart	host	lad	nine	nun
hearts	hot	leach	nines	nunnery
heat	hots	lead	nit	nuns
heats	hotter	load	nits	nurse
heed	hug	loaded	no	oar
held	ice	loo	nod	oars
her	ices	loom	nog	oat
hero	icon	loon	noise	oath
heros	icons	mm	none	oaths
hers	in	mold	noo	oats
he's	inch	mom	noon	odd
ho	ingest	moo	noose	ode
hog	inn	mood	nos	oh
hold	inns	moon	nosing	old
hole	ins	neon	nosy	om
holed	insect	neons	not	on

once	rates	rot	share	so
one	rather	rotate	sharer	soar
ones	rats	rotates	shatter	soarer
onion	rear	rots	she	son
onions	rears	run	shear	song
onset	reshoot	runs	shoe	sonnet
onto	reshot	rye	shoot	soon
ooh	resort	sat	shooter	soot
oohs	rest	scent	shore	sooth
or	restart	scone	short	soothe
other	retro	scoot	shorter	soother
others	roar	scooting	shot	sore
otter	roars	sea	siege	sort
otters	roast	seat	sign	sorter
ouch	roaster	section	sin	sour
our	roost	see	since	soy
ours	rooster	seeing	sing	star
rare	root	seen	sit	stare
rarest	roots	seize	site	starer
rash	rose	sent	size	start
rat	roster	set	snoot	starter
rate	rosy	sh	snore	state

sting	the	tonics	yes
stone	those	toning	yo
store	threat	tons	you
sue	threats	too	your
sun	throat	toon	yours
sunny	tic	toons	yous
sure	tics	toot	zee
tar	tie	tooth	zees
tart	ties	torso	zen
tarts	tin	tot	zig
taste	tins	tots	zigs
taster	to	trash	zing
tea	toast	treat	
tear	toaster	treats	
tears	toe	trot	
teas	toes	ugh	
teat	ton	uh	
ten	tone	urn	
tennis	tones	urns	
tension	tong	us	
test	tongs	use	
that	tonic	user	

Printed in Great Britain
by Amazon

39931167R00023